ISBN-13: 9798362801168

Cover design by: J.A. Rainbow
Library of Congress Control Number: 2018675309
Printed in the United Kingdom

Thanks go, as always, to my wonderful wife Laura, also to our niece Rachel who requested a festive story and to both of them who found it hilarious that I was once a Santa's elf!

This book is for Lucas

Contents

Chapter 1

It was the week before Christmas and snow was falling in Glasgow. Lights twinkled from trees in windows and gardens were decorated with fake Santas and inflatable snowmen. People bustled up and down Buchanan Street maniacally buying bright coloured gifts, dressed in Christmas jumpers and dodging the slightly tipsy office workers out on their staff do.

Ellie and Kate had been in every shop…twice. They almost fell through their front door in exhaustion, Ellie carrying all the bags and Kate limping behind her with her stick. Peggy was sitting in the living room watching 'Die hard' and was half way through a tin of Quality Street.

"Do you ever go home?" quipped Ellie as she dumped the bags by the door and stretched her back.

"With the price of gas and leccy these days? No chance, I'll sponge off you two." Peggy muttered as she paused her film and got up to help Kate with some of the bags. "Anyway how was your shopping trip?"

"Absolutely mental" groaned Ellie as she kicked off her boots. "Your niece got into a fight with a woman over a jumper in John Lewis."

"It was *cashmere*" Kate said as if that justified the fight.

"I know honey but there were five more of them on the table behind you, there was no need to push the poor woman against the wall by her throat!"

"That one was the perfect colour to match mum's eyes" Kate growled as she went through to the kitchen to make tea.

"It was the same colour as the others..." Ellie whispered to Peggy as the older woman shrugged in their shared confusion.

"They were *not* the same Eleanor Mitchell-McVey!" Kate bellowed from the kitchen.

"So what have you been up to today Peggy?" Ellie asked, changing the subject.

"Well I attempted to take your dogs out for a walk but we got as far as the front garden. Bruiser dived head first into a snow pile that attached to his fur like giant snowballs and Bella put one paw out into the snow and bolted back into the house. He's asleep by the radiator to dry off and she's still traumatised and in a huff on that chair." Peggy explained pointing to the old Westie giving them stink eye from her perch by the fire, clearly still affronted at being made to go out in snow.

"When is mum home from Santa's grotto?" Kate asked as she came in and slumped on the couch. Bella deigned to leave her chair to jump up beside Kate for a belly rub.

"She should be here any minute, then we'll get that tree up and decorated eh?" Peggy said checking her watch.

Aggie came in dressed as Mrs Claus and dropped her bag at the door. She had volunteered to be a part of Santa's grotto at the local community centre. It was a free event to help struggling families get a bit of festive cheer, a mince pie and a present for a child that would not be getting much this year. Ellie had roped the station in and there was a pile of donated toys and warm clothes ready to be delivered to the grotto.

"How was it today Mrs Claus?" Peggy asked.

"Better, only two kiddies cried when they got to Santa today and they all looked dead happy when they got presents, bless them. Why isn't the tree up yet?" she asked pointing to the assorted boxes that contained the fake tree and all the decorations."

"We were waiting for you, if you remember the last time I tried to decorate it without you, you made me re-do the whole bloody thing?" Peggy said.

"Oh for the love of…that was twenty years ago woman! And I should hope you know how to do it properly by now." Aggie grumbled as she went to get changed.

"How have you got clothes here? Do you ever go home?" Ellie asked for the second time that day.

"What? With electricity being what it is and me a pensioner? No I'll stay here ta." Aggie said and Peggy grinned as Ellie shook her head at the pair of them.

They spent the evening decorating the tree, putting tinsel up and laughing at stories of Christmases when Kate was a child. Peggy had cracked open a bottle of Baileys and they all sat round the tree pleased with the evening's work.

"What did you get me for Christmas?" Peggy asked suddenly but no one answered. She had been asking the same question at least four times a day for the past month in the hope that someone would give in and tell her.

"Peggy if you ask me that one more time I'm sending it bloody back!" Aggie said, her faced flushed with her third glass.

"Peggy, considering what you do for a living, I'm surprised you need to ask us. Surely you have ways of finding out." Ellie teased knowing full well that Aggie and Kate had prepared with military precision this year, no paper trail and cash purchases. Presents hidden at a secure location known only to them (Ellie was an information casualty in case Peggy broke her).

Chapter 2

"Thanks for giving me a lift Ellie dear" Aggie said quietly from the passenger seat. Ellie smiled, Aggie was currently suffering from a gale force hangover after she and Peggy 'made a night of it' on mulled wine after finishing the Baileys.

"Not a problem, I'm dropping our donations off anyway… besides I think you still have too much booze in your blood to be driving anywhere." Ellie joked.

"I am not hungover…it's a headache…from stress… Christmas and all that…" Aggie muttered as she rubbed her temples "Is there any way you could drive in a direction that wasn't in direct sunlight?"

"Afraid not, here put these sunglasses on" Ellie rummaged down the side of her door and pulled out some glasses that Aggie took gratefully.

They parked outside the community centre and Aggie made her way in to take her position as Mrs Claus. Ellie opened the boot of the car and started to lift out bags and boxes full of toys and clothes. When she made her way inside Aggie was standing beside Santa and pointed at her. Santa bounded over to her jovially and shook her free hand.

"Your mother-in-law said you would be coming, very

pleased to meet you and thank you and your colleagues for the generous donations." He said all this while still pumping Ellie's hand up and down.

"Ah Ellie this is Ron Casey, our Santa." Aggie added, as if the red suit, portly frame and white beard needed this explanation.

"Pleased to meet you Ron." Ellie said as she managed to wrangle her hand free. "It's good of you to give up your time like this."

"Oh nonsense, what else would I do with my time? I'm retired you know, school janitor for years amongst other things…no I like to get out amongst folk and keep active. Well I can't stand about, it's nearly showtime. Nice to meet you though." he said as he bounded off towards his chair in the grotto.

"He's…enthusiastic?" Ellie said and Aggie smiled.

"He can be a bit…but he's really good with the kids and has done a lot of the fundraising for this himself. He's a good man." Aggies explained before heading back to join Santa as the punters started to file in.

Ellie was stacking up all the donations on a trestle table at the other end of the hall, her back to the grotto so that the kids couldn't see the presents as she piled them up and draped blankets over the mounds.

All of a sudden there was a loud crash and a scream from behind her, she spun round to see chaos. A light fixture had fallen and just missed Santa's chair and Santa himself. Kids were crying and Santa was clutching at his chest as Mrs Claus was fanning a fainting mother with her wig. Ellie ran over to calm things down and usher the kiddies away.

"What happened?" she asked as she bodily lifted the unconscious mother off Aggie.

"Oh that bloody light fell and nearly killed us all! Thankfully no one was hurt, this one is just being melodramatic" she nudged the woman with her toe.

"Fixture must have been loose." muttered Ellie as she looked at the light on the floor.

"Never, I wired those up myself young lady and I've been doing that since before you were born!" Ron/Santa piped up, regaining some of his ruddy complexion.

"Well it wasn't the pixies Ron" Aggie snapped. "Anyone can make a mistake"

"I didn't make a bloody mistake woman! You could have swung on those lights they were that secure!" Ron snapped back, affronted at the accusation that he was inept at electrics.

"Look you two it doesn't matter whose fault it is!" bellowed Ellie. "No one was hurt and thankfully no damage done. So how about we get this lot cleared up and calm down and then try to bring some cheer to folk eh?" she pacified them as the Christmas spouses looked fit for a quick divorce.

"Sorry Ellie dear...I must admit I'm on edge, the elves are having rows with Santa and now this..." Aggie muttered as she walked away.

<h1 style="text-align:center">Chapter 3</h1>

Kate had spent the morning making mince pies, she had to do a lot of it sitting down these days but she enjoyed baking them. As she walked into the living room she spotted Peggy standing at the window with her arms folded, glaring out.

"What are you watching?" Kate asked as she walked towards the window.

"Him" muttered Peggy. Kate followed her line of vision to a small boy running about outside.

"Why are you watching a wean running about?"

"Look at him, he's a little thug!" Peggy said as they watched him throwing snowballs at peoples windows and passing cars.

"Kids today have no discipline… I'm not having that wee tearaway giving the street a bad name" she muttered as she rapped the window with her knuckles. The boy looked over and then with a malevolent grin pelted a snowball straight at the window and gave Peggy the finger and ran off.

"Honestly when did people stop using the good old 'v sign'" she huffed. "I'm going out to have words with that boy" she started but Kate stepped in front of her and shoved a mince pie in her mouth.

"Calm down Peggy, he's a kid and it's Christmas. Come on, I'll get you some mulled wine, that will cheer you up."

Peggy grudgingly moved away from the target of her vexation and followed Kate to the kitchen. Aggie came home at this point looking a bit flustered and Peggy took the opportunity to resume her position at the window (albeit now with a mulled wine in hand) as Kate asked Aggie what was wrong.

"Oh nothing...well something...oh I don't know Katie." Aggie babbled.

"Mum sit down and explain." Kate said gently as she led Aggie to the couch.

"Well there was an accident at the grotto this morning, a light fell but no one was hurt thankfully...but I'm beginning to worry that it wasn't an accident."

"Why do you think it wasn't?"

"Ron is adamant that he personally fixed that light up and is sure that he did it securely. He's a fastidious man, unlikely to make a mistake with safety."

"But why would someone do it on purpose?" Kate asked. "I mean it's a charity Santa's grotto."

"I don't know love...but it's a feeling that isn't going away and I don't know what to do to shake it."

"Why don't I ask Ellie to look into it?"

"Oh no...no I don't want to bother her with this, I'm probably just imagining it. It's just that there's so much bickering among the volunteers. I wish I could just figure out what was going on and then it would settle my mind a bit." Aggie admitted.

"So what you need is someone on the inside to keep an eye on things…" Kate said quietly as a plan to kill two birds with one stone emerged. "I think I know just the person" she said with a smile as she watched Peggy giving the 'v sign' out the window as another snowball struck the pane.

Chapter 4

Gavin parked a van borrowed from his mate, in front of the community centre. He is delivering the rest of the donations from the officers at the station. He, Ellie and Kate are working together to carry bags full of gifts through to a small room at the back of the hall as there was now too many things to hide under a blanket on a table. After a couple of trips Gavin stopped and watched the action at the grotto for a moment.

"Who's idea was that again?" he asked.

"Mine" replied Kate.

"And why did we think it was a *good* idea?" he carried on, still watching the grotto.

"Oi, any more of that and you're out!" bellowed the voice from the grotto.

"Her work have made her take her holiday leave or she loses it in January, if she sat in our house for all that time she would kill the neighbourhood kids in a week" Kate explained.

"And you thought this would be better..." Gavin responded still watching as Peggy marched up and down the line of waiting children, the bells on her elf shoes ringing as she went. She looked like the drill sergeant of a newly formed

Elf Military force.

"She'll be fine" Kate said waiving her hand dismissively.

"She's searching their bags!" Gavin said pointing to the fiasco.

Ellie joined his vigil and watched as Peggy marched back to the head of the queue as a young boy came out from seeing Santa, clutching his gift cheerfully as he ran towards his dad.

"Right, who's next…" Peggy looked to the boy in front. "Not you young man, I saw you kicking your sister when you thought no one was looking, she gets to go ahead of you."

Like a bouncer at a city centre nightclub, Peggy opened up the rope at the start of the queue and ushered the boy's sister through before closing it again and crossing her arms over her chest, her foot tapping and jingling the bells.

"Yeah…best not to watch anymore of this…" Ellie said quietly as she patted Gavin on the shoulder.

"She'll be fine, she will get used to it" Kate replied "Come on, we've still got loads of boxes in that van. We're cutting it fine for you two to get to work".

Chapter 5

When the last of the children leave, Aggie and Ron stand up and stretch, stiff from sitting for so long.

"Busy one today" Ron said as he cracked his back.

"It was, but those kids looked so happy." Aggie responded.

"Well they were once they got past that new volunteer, what's her name again? Mavis?"

"Margaret" Aggie corrected him, she had neglected to tell anyone that Peggy was her sister, that way she could nose about more efficiently.

"Margaret yes that's right, odd woman don't you think?" Ron mused.

"Can't say I've noticed" Aggie replied as evenly as she could.

"Hmm, well…just feel there's something funny about her. I mean, she doesn't really feel like the volunteer with children type. But maybe it's just me" Ron said jovially as Aggie was not responding to his prompts to gossip.

"Well I think it was very nice of her to volunteer at the last minute for a worthy cause. I'd better get ready to leave." She said as she walked towards the coat hook.

"Aren't you going into the cloakroom to get changed?" Ron asked.

"No, I prefer to launder these outfits at night, keep them fresh."

Peggy had walked quietly into the cloakroom and positioned herself around the corner so that no one could see her hidden behind coats and bags. She had chatted to the other volunteers throughout the day to make sure they all realised that she was friendly, approachable and up for a gossip. She had agreed with Aggie prior to starting that she should make up some tale about Aggie, just to see if that would ingratiate her with the rest of the volunteers. It seemed to work well and the others were less guarded around her. Some of the other volunteers were already in the cloakroom getting changed when she slipped herself onto a bench to listen on the pretence of changing.

"Did you see him today nearly having a heart attack when that light fell? Honestly I nearly wet myself!" said one of the female voices as she chuckled.

'Sounds like Vikki' thought Peggy as she took time lacing up her winter boots.

"Aye, must admit I had a laugh myself. Took the pompous look off his face for a minute eh?" the second voice added with a cackle.

'Sandra' thought Peggy.

"I mean I don't get how he got picked to be the Santa anyway, he's been a mean old bugger all his days." Sandra continued.

"Really? I just thought he became a crabbit aul' git with age." Vikki said.

"Nope, always was mean spirited that one."

"How do you know?" Vikki responded.

"Friend of mine worked with him for years, school janitor, the weans hated him apparently."

Peggy was filing this little nugget away when the door crashed open and Annie waddled through, in her haste she missed Peggy completely and rounded the corner to the others.

"Oh thank god you lot are still here, give us a hand eh? The zip on this bloody costume is stuck again and I'm not getting on that bus dressed as a snowman again! It brings the worst out of the weirdos on that night bus." She complained as Sandra yanked at the zip to get it unstuck. It unjammed in a few seconds and Annie was free.

"Oh ta, that's saved me a bit of stress. You two leaving? I still need to change."

"Aye hen, we need to get on but we'll see you tomorrow eh?" Vikki responded.

Peggy made her exit quickly so that they wouldn't spot her on their way out. She had agreed to meet up with Aggie outside, she made her way out to the frigid night air and looked around, Aggie waived discreetly at her from outside the shop across the road. Peggy joined her sister and started to walk towards her car that was parked further up the road.

"Were you waiting long?" asked Peggy.

"No dear I'm just out. I needed to get away from Ron, he's fishing for gossip about you."

"Ah, I've made an impression then" Peggy smiled.

"Don't you always Peggy dear?"

"Where is Ron anyway? Is he not usually first out the door?" Peggy asked as she looked back towards the centre.

"Aye usually he is, said he needed to check something though. He's got keys to lock up anyway. The heating better be fixed in that car of yours Peggy, my feet might have dropped off already and I'm too cold to notice."

"Yes I got big Alan to have a look at it the other day."

"Big Alan the convicted joyrider?" Aggie groaned.

"That was when he was wee Alan, since he got with that lassie he's matured, uses his skills to fix cars instead of nicking them."

"Honestly Peggy, the amount if dodgy people that you know, you'd never think you worked for the Government."

"Shhh Aggie the world doesn't need to know that. Besides, shady people are sometimes the best people to know when you're in trouble and are usually more honest." Peggy responded simply. "You try getting a mechanic to fix the heating in your car for nothing more than a crate of beer".

Chapter 6

Ellie arrives home just after 5pm, Kate is surprised, she's never that early.

"Not busy at work then?" she asked as she kissed Ellie in greeting.

"Nope, looks like the criminals of Glasgow have taken the festive season off, hopefully it continues. I've sent the team home early and I'm on call just in case anything happens. Gavin is heading home to start tackling the twins Christmas presents. Apparently, Mhairi has bought a lot of toys that require building" Ellie said with a chuckle.

"Poor Gavin, it'll take him ages. Did you not offer to help?"

"I did, but he said with my clumsiness I would be more of a hindrance than a help…rude" she muttered but Kate smiled, he wasn't wrong.

"So, as I'm home at a respectable hour for once, is there any late-night shopping needing done for presents?" she asked.

"I don't think so, I'm pretty sure we've got something for everyone plus I've bought in tins of sweets and bottles of wine for emergency gifts." Kate explained as she plonked herself down on the couch and changed the tv channel.

"Emergency gifts?" Ellie looked puzzled.

"Yes, gifts for unexpected people, you know when you go

somewhere and there's some friend of a friend that shows up with a gift for you and you've not got them anything? Well, I keep emergency gifts in the boot of the car and in the spare room for such occasions." Kate explained as if this was the most logical thing in the world. Ellie had never thought that far ahead when it came to gift giving, she bought for her close group, and it was cards for everyone else.

They spent a quiet couple of hours watching some Christmas specials of sitcoms until Peggy and Aggie walked through the door, Peggy was furious and swearing profusely as she stormed in and went straight to the window. Aggie filled them in on what had happened.

"Young Marcus from across the street chucked a snowball at her, it went down her neck."

"Marcus? That's his name, is it? Little beggar! I don't know what kids are at these days, but I'll get him for this, oh yes mark my words, I'll get him." Peggy threatened, her eyes still fixed outside as her target, Marcus gleefully ran about ignorant of his new nemesis plotting against him.

"So how did it go today?" Kate asked, desperate to change the subject. It seemed to work as Peggy finally pulled away from the window and sat down in the armchair near the fire.

"It went very well, once the children learned the rules of queuing." Peggy replied and Ellie snorted, she managed to change it into a cough before Peggy noticed.

"What about the volunteers, did you get any impression that one of them is up to no good?" Kate asked.

"I wouldn't say anyone was up to anything, but I can say that a few of them really don't like that bloke that plays Santa, they were giving him a right slagging in the cloakroom today. They were questioning his suitability to play Santa; say he's always been a mean old sod."

"Well, there's no law against not liking someone. I would hate to think of what my team call me on a bad day" Ellie said.

"Does that help settle your mind mum?" Kate asked.

"A little, I'm just happy that Peggy is there, I feel a little calmer with her around just in case." Aggie admitted.

"I bet the kids are really pleased she's there too." muttered Ellie as Kate elbowed her in the ribs.

"What was that Ellie?" Peggy asked sharply.

"Nothing, shall I make some tea?" Ellie said quickly as she scarpered to the kitchen.

Chapter 7

The next morning, Kate is packing her bag for the day. She was asked to take part in a celebrity choir to raise money for local charities and their final practice was this morning.

"When is your first gig?" Ellie asked as she filled her travel mug with coffee.

"It's not a gig, choirs don't have gigs, it's a performance. It's tomorrow at the St Enoch Centre. Oh and I've managed to arrange for mum's grotto to volunteer to be there and dish out some gifts and sweets to kids while we sing. The shopping centre had scenery we could use sitting in storage so I think the whole thing will be really festive." Kate said brightly as she stole Ellie's coffee mug, kissed her goodbye and left the house before Ellie could register what happened.

Ellie shook her head and went back to the kitchen to make up another travel cup and headed to work.

She got to the office to find Gavin in full decorating mode, he had roped Kent and Simpson in too. They were singing along to the Christmas hits cd that Gavin had been using for years and played the usual Christmas pop hits. Ellie watched from the door amused as they draped tinsel over every available space, every desk, pc, picture frame even the murder board got a festive upgrade. Gavin was getting very into his rendition of 'Santa Baby' which part amused and part horrified his audience. Ellie slipped quietly in and put some gifts for each of the team under their little office tree. Lights were twinkling from various places in the office and Ellie had to admit that Gavin and the rest of the team had made a normally grim room, very cheery. She watched them decorate for a while and then, during a very enthusiastic chorus of "fiiiiive goooooolllllld riiiiiiiings!!!" the phone rang. Ellie jumped up to answer it as the others calmed down their exuberant singing once they noticed she was there…well everyone except Gavin.

"Murder and serious crime squad, Detective Superintendent McVey speaking." Ellie answered the phone as she mouthed to Kent to turn the music down a little bit.

"Good morning Ma'am, this is PC Dukar from Community Policing…um…a member of the public flagged me down this morning in a bit of a state. He said he found a body." Dukar explained.

"Ok, give me the details and we'll get over there." Ellie said grabbing a pen.

"Well Ma'am it's a bit of a strange one…you see Santa's dead."

"Excuse me?" Ellie asked as her pen hovered after that last remark.

"The Santa at Maryhill community halls ma'am" Dukar explained. "He was found dead this morning. My Sergeant said I was to notify you and Doctor Brett."

"Thank you, we're on our way, make sure that area stays sealed." Ellie instructed as she hung up the phone.

"I take it that our easy Christmas is cancelled?" Gavin asked as he got off a stool where he was pinning up some mistletoe.

"It is, and take that down! I'm not having a repeat of last year with half the admin staff hanging about under that stuff waiting for you to pass by like teenagers at a boy band's hotel!" Ellie rolled her eyes. "We've got a body…and I think it's Ron."

"Santa Ron?" Gavin asked.

"The very same" Ellie responded.

"Hang on….Santa's dead?" Simpson asked in confusion.

Chapter 8

Ellie and Gavin arrive at the community centre once more but this time as a crime scene. Doc Brett was already on scene, her covered shoes moving around the body scanning for every injury. Ellie focused on the body. Ron was still in his Santa gear, he was lying on his front beside a toppled ladder. There was blood pooling beneath him.

"Morning Doc, what have you got for me?" Ellie asked as she pulled gloves on.

"Morning yourself, I'm supposed to be on my way to the Christmas market with the in-laws this morning...so I must say this Santa corpse isn't the worst bit of my day!" Doc admitted as she made notes on her tablet. "Time of death was some time last night, between 6pm and 10pm, sorry I can't be more specific at the moment. Cause of death appears to be blunt force trauma to the skull but I'll know more after the post mortem." She explained.

"So do we think he fell off the ladder and conked his head?" Gavin asked as he looked at the ladder.

"You know I won't guess" sang Doc Brett as she finished making notes.

"What was he doing up a ladder anyway? I mean he wasn't

exactly in the fullness of youth was he?" Gavin muttered as Ellie looked up to the ceiling from where the ladder was.

"Look, if you were to stand that ladder back up, it would be under that dodgy bit of light rigging that nearly killed him. Do you think he was up fixing it?" she pondered.

"Well he was a jannie wasn't he? He probably spent half his working life up ladders fixing stuff in schools." Gavin conceded. "So accidental death?"

"Probably…but let's work the scene as a crime until we know for sure." Ellie decided.

"You're the boss…so what's the plan?"

"We need to interview the volunteers, establish a timeline and possible alibis just in case." Ellie said as she listed off what needed to be done. "If Doc is right about time of death then Aggie and Peggy were already home before he died so we don't need to worry about any conflict of interest that might arise from them."

As if they knew they were being discussed, Peggy's voice could be heard from the entrance to the halls.

"What do you mean we can't go in? What's going on?" she thundered.

"Damage control" whispered Ellie and Gavin nodded as he went out to talk to Peggy.

"Ah young Gavin, what's going on?" Aggie asked as he headed their direction.

"Come with me and don't say anything" he whispered as he pulled them into a side room.

"Right you two, Ellie will be here in a minute but I need to fill you in on what's happened. Ron's been found dead this morning…"

"Oh no that poor man…"exclaimed Aggie as her hands covered her face.

"What happened?" Peggy asked seriously as she patted her sisters shoulder in a comforting gesture.

"It looks like he fell off a ladder and banged his head but we'll know more soon." Gavin explained as Ellie came in and closed the door.

"So Ron's dead…sorry Aggie…until we know more, we're treating this as a crime scene. I'd like to ask both of you to carry on as if you don't know each other and Peggy you don't know us. Just for now…"

"Do you think you might need us to snoop?" Peggy asked.

"I don't know, but I'd rather keep the option. So if any of the others ask, you were in here being asked your whereabouts last night." Ellie told them and they nodded their understanding.

"Was it an accident?" Aggie asked, sniffling a little bit.

"It's looking that way but we really don't know. Forensics are going over the place just now and Doc Brett will do the post today and let us know for sure. I think it would be best if you both went home though, this place will be shut for the day and there's nothing you can do here."

"Of course…you're right. We'll head home…but tell us if you know anything?" Aggie replied.

"Of course."

"Honestly though, I can't see anyone wanting to kill Santa the week before Christmas." Gavin soothed.

Chapter 9

Ellie and Gavin bring some chairs and a table into the side room that they had used to talk to Peggy and Aggie. They decided that it was a good place to interview the rest of the volunteers as they were all standing around anyway. Ellie instructed the PC standing by the door to bring in the person who found the body and then she got prepared. They didn't have to wait long before an older gentleman started to shuffle through, only he stopped and whispered something to the PC who nodded and the man shuffled off.

"What's the hold up?" Ellie asked.

"He needs a wee" the officer responded.

"Oh well, we may as well get his information off you before he comes back. What do we know about him?" Ellie asked.

"He's the cleaner, Ernie Pritchard."

"Cleaner? What's that poor old soul doing working at his time of life?" Gavin asked, looking sad.

"Don't feel sorry for him Sir, he owned his own building company for years, he sold it for millions when he retired. He started up a cleaning company for something to do" the officer explained as they watched Ernie's slow, stooped progression back towards them.

"Worth millions? He looks like he's carrying it on his back!" Gavin exclaimed as he watched the multi-millionaire slowly walk through the door and sit down.

"So sorry about that…my bladder isn't what it used to be" Ernie explained.

"That's alright Mr Pritchard, we will try not to keep you too long, we just have a few questions." Ellie responded kindly. "Firstly, can you tell us about the events of this morning?"

"Oh yes, well I arrived to do my cleaning shift at the usual time, I'm always here for 7am, I'm an early riser you see. It's all those years as a builder that's done it. Anyway, I usually have my nephew with me for this job but he's away on some stag-do so it was just me today. I went to open; but the door was already open." Ernie explained.

"Is that normal?" Ellie asked.

"It happens from time to time, Ron's an early riser like me, sometimes he would come in early and brew up and we'd have a cuppa together. He would even push a mop about the place if his lumbago wasn't playing up."

"So you didn't think this was odd, that's fine, please continue" Ellie said.

"So I walked through the door and called his name, but he didn't answer. I thought he might have been at the loo or something, so I went to the cleaning cupboard, hung up my coat and got the hoover out. It was only when I walked into the main hall that I noticed him." Ernie said quietly.

"I know it must have been distressing but can you explain what you saw?"

"I wasn't distressed, sadly in my profession I saw industrial accidents that would turn your hair white. I went into the hall and saw Ron lying on his front."

"Did you move him or touch him?" Gavin asked.

"I took his pulse but other than that, no I didn't move him. My wife watches 'silent witness' so I know enough to not move him."

"So you found Ron, went to take his pulse, then what?" Ellie asked.

"I tried to phone the police, knew it was too late for an ambulance, the poor sod was cold. But my phone battery died so I ran outside and flagged down a local polis. He called it in and then I waited for you lot to show up."

"Can you describe what was around him?" Ellie asked.

"Aye…the ladder was on its side, his Santa parcel bag was lying to its side, even his Santa bell had rolled away into the middle of the floor. He must have landed with some thump." Ernie said shaking his head. "I saw blood on his head and underneath him too."

"Thanks for that Ernie, we just needed to make sure that the scene we saw was the same one that you saw. Just in case anyone moved anything after the fact." Ellie explained without trying to make it sound like she was accusing him of tampering with a crime scene. "We think he died early last night, can you tell me about your whereabouts for the evening?"

"Alibi you mean?" Ernie asked surprised.

"Just for our records, we don't imagine anything untoward has happened, but we need to cover all the bases".

"Oh, that's ok, wait until I tell the wife that I needed to have an alibi! She'll be so jealous!" Ernie was gleeful at the prospect for a moment. "Oh yes, sorry…ahem…time and a place, eh? Yesterday evening was my great grandson's nativity play at his school. I watched that and then we all went out for a family dinner. He was a T-Rex you know…not quite sure when T-Rexs made an appearance at the nativity but there you are." Ernie said shrugging his shoulders.

"Thank you, Mr Pritchard; I think that's all we need for now. If we need any more information we'll be in touch, but if you can think of anything that might be useful, please give us a call." Ellie said standing up and handing Ernie a business card with her number on it.

"Oh of course, anything I can do to help" he said cheerfully. By the time Ernie Pritchard left the room he looked like a younger man…he looked like someone with only half a million being carried on his back.

<h1 style="text-align:center">Chapter 10</h1>

Kate comes home from choir practice, surprised to find Aggie and Peggy at home. Aggie can be heard chatting to one of her friends on the phone in the kitchen, and Peggy was standing once again at the window, with a malevolent glare on her face and a piece of toast in her hand.

"Shouldn't you be spreading joy to all the dear little children by now?" Kate quipped as she hung up her coat.

"Can't, Santa's dead and Ellie's closed the Grotto as a crime scene" Peggy explained as she munched on her toast. "Ellie and young Gavin are down there interviewing the volunteers, so they told us to scarper for the day" Peggy continued, her eyes never leaving the window.

"What are you looking at?" Kate asked suspiciously as she joined Peggy at the window. She watched as Marcus ran about pelting passers-by with snowballs. She also watched him being chased out of the neighbour's gardens as he continued his one-man assault on the neighbourhood. Kate looked around and was surprised to see Peggy smiling.

"Why are you smiling? I know that smile, it's your victory smile, you use it when you play monopoly..."

"I don't know what you mean, am I not allowed to smile these days...oh by the way, I went out and washed the path earlier. The steps were fine but there was an awful lot of grit on the pavement outside, so I had to use a lot of water to wash it away" Peggy commented innocently as she continued her vigil.

"Water? Peggy it's minus 3 outside! Someone will have a fall! In fact if I had walked that way I would have copped it!"

Just as she said it, there was a howl from outside. Marcus had coming running round from next door's garden giving the 'v sign' to old Mrs Wilson and slipped on the icy path and went clattering into the fence. Kate watched as his mum ran out and picked him up and took him inside. Peggy looked positively triumphant.

"Peggy! You evil scrooge-like..." Kate began.

"What? I'm not psychic! How could I have possibly predicted that the dear little boy would have such an accident? What a shame...oh and don't look at me like that, I'll go grit the pavement again... by the way Katie, did I tell you I've been promoted from elf?" Peggy said lightly, changing the subject as she went to sit on the couch.

"Really, what's your new title? Chief Executioner?" Kate grumbled but Peggy ignored her.

"No dear, my talent has been spotted and put to better use. I'm to be the new Santa" she said with a grin. Kate stood in shocked silence.

"The man's only just died! How has there already been a discussion about you taking over?"

"That Vikki one called Aggie half an hour ago and told her there needed to be a decision so as not to disappoint the kids tomorrow." Peggy explained.

"She's only Santa because no other bugger is daft enough to

do it! Everyone else thinks the job is jinxed" Aggie said as she came through. "Besides, I think there was about to be complaints from the parents. This one was issuing threats of waterboarding in the queue."

"Honestly…you make *one* wee threat" Peggy muttered.

Chapter 11

Back at the community centre Gavin enters the room carrying coffee.

"There you go boss lady, I got you one of those cinnamon spice coffee things that you like." He explained as he sat a festive looking paper coffee cup in front of her.

"Life saver" she groaned. "Who have we got next?"

"One of the elves…um…" Gavin checked his notes. "Robbie Banks, age 28 and according to some quick searching by Kent, he went to the same school that Ron was the Janny at."

"Interesting, well that will be one of the first things we ask him. Bring him in, and is there no heating in this place?" she asked as she pulled her coat tighter around her.

"Yeah I asked about that…it would appear that the menopausal ladies rule the thermostat in this place. I tried to turn the heating on and got my hand slapped by some 4ft tall Lilliputian called Iris who told me to put a jumper on if I was cold. She reminded me of one of my granny's sisters." He said with a smile.

"Great we'll just get a door and do our Jack and Rose off the titanic and bloody freeze to death." Ellie muttered. She hated being cold.

Robbie Banks came in behind Gavin, the bells on his elf shoes jingling as he walked.

"Sorry about the noise, I came here in my costume so I can't change." He explained apologetically. He was a large man, almost Gavin's build with dark hair and a small scar on his left cheek. He folded his large frame into the chair opposite Ellie and smiled, waiting for her to begin.

"Thank you for coming to talk to us Robbie. I think the first question we have is, did you know Ron before volunteering here?" Ellie asked.

"Oh aye, I've known auld Ron since I was a wean. He was the janny at my school." Robbie said cheerfully.

"Did you have many dealings with him back then?" Ellie asked, suspicious of Robbie's cheery disposition given the circumstances. That question seemed to break the spell as Robbie's face fell a little.

"Ah…so you know about that then." He said quietly. Ellie had no clue what he was talking about and the shrug Gavin gave her behind Robbie's back indicated that he didn't either.

"Yes…yes we know about it Robbie but we wanted to give you the opportunity of telling us about it in your own words." Ellie said calmly, hoping that was the correct response to get him talking.

"Aye fair enough…well as you know, I was expelled from school at 15, I was caught nicking wallets from the teachers break room…it was auld Ron that caught me in the act. He went through me, read me the riot act and gave me a slap round the head. He marched me to the head's office and I was expelled."

"That must have made you very angry" Gavin said quietly.

"Aye it did, but I was 15 man, everything made me angry. Ron said to me that Rob Banks wasn't my name it was my future. It took me a few years and a lot of maturing before I realised that he was right. I went into the army at 18 and they straightened me out, I made something of myself... had I not been caught and kicked out when I was, I probably would have ended up robbing banks." He chuckled sadly. "I know what you're thinking, that I wanted revenge on Ron...but I don't hold a grudge against him at all. In fact he's the reason I ended up volunteering here, I wanted to give back to my community and to show the auld fella that I had made a good life."

"Admirable" Ellie said without irony. "I need to ask though, where were you last night?"

"Well let's see...I finished my shift here and then I met up with a few pals I used to run about with...a wee festive drink. We ended up at the horseshoe bar down the road until about 11 and then I went home."

"That's great, one final question, did you know if Ron was having any trouble?"

"Um...I don't think so, I doubt he would say even if he was to be fair." Robbie said with a shrug.

"Ok, that's all for now, we'll be in touch if there's anything more we need." Ellie said as he got up and shook her hand before leaving the room.

Chapter 12

A stout woman with grey streaks in her dark hair was next through the door for Ellie and Gavin.

"This is Annie Wilkins Ma'am" the young PC stated as he showed her to her seat.

"Good morning Annie, we won't take up much of your time, we know today has been a bit of a shock" Ellie started gently as Annie was sniffling into a hanky.

"Yes...a shock...poor Ron..." Annie managed before sobbing.

"Can you tell us what your role is here?" Ellie decided to ease the woman in gently.

"I'm the snowman...or snowwoman? I um...well I kind of just wander about shaking hands with the kiddies and getting photos taken while they wait. It's... um...just something to get me out of the house really." She said quietly. "I made my costume myself" she said with pride, her face brightening a little.

"I'm sure the kids love it." Gavin said kindly and she smiled at him.

"Now can you tell us what you did when you left here last night?"

"Well…it took me longer than usual to leave…I got stuck in my snowman suit…the zip needed fixing you see. So I got the girls to help me out of it and then I headed out for my bus."

"Did you see Ron before you left?" Ellie asked.

"Yes I did, he helped me carry my bag of messages out to the bus stop, kind man that he was…" she started sobbing again.

"So…you're saying Ron left when you did?" Ellie asked.

"Oh no…no he carried my shopping out and then went back into the community centre…said he was wanting to check something before he left."

"Ah I see, and was anyone else there when you left?" Ellie continued.

"Um…oh I don't know dear…I don't remember seeing anyone but I wasn't really paying attention, I was worried about catching my bus, getting out of my costume made me late."

"And you went straight home?"

"Oh yes, I don't stay out after dark…the teenagers at my bit are feral wee hooligans so I get in and lock the door. I spent the night fixing the zip on my costume and I watched a lovely wee film." She said with a smile.

"A Christmas film?" Ellie asked.

"Naw…last tango in Paris" Annie said with a sigh. Ellie was sorry she asked.

Chapter 13

Ellie's head was on the desk as she gave herself a few minutes before the next volunteer to be interviewed. Her head was pounding, she was convinced that the frigid air in here was to blame somehow.

"Who do we have next Gav?" she muttered into the desk.

"Sandra Cullen, another elf and I think this is the one Peggy told us was complaining about Ron in the changing room." He responded from deep inside his scarf, only his eyes were visible now.

"Ah ok, we'll keep that wee bit of info until after we've asked her opinion of him." Ellie decided as she sat up, instantly regretting her change in equilibrium.

"You got any painkillers in your bag?" she asked as she pinched the bridge of her nose.

"I do, but you should be wearing your glasses." he told her as he fished a packet of Nurofen out of his bag.

"It's my sinuses not my eyes." She muttered. "Besides they're reading glasses and I'm not currently reading am I?" Gavin had been teasing her ever since she turned 40 that she was falling apart, the news that she now needed reading glasses seemed to justify his theory.

"As soon as we get out of here and thaw out I'll be fine" she muttered.

"Ach look on the bright side Els, you're only about five years away from the old Peri-menopause yourself so you will start to love arctic temperatures." Gavin quipped as he ducked the packet of painkillers that were aimed at his head.

"Your wife is six weeks older than me, somehow I doubt she would be very happy to hear you talk like this…so not one more word or I'm telling" Ellie threatened. That did the trick, Gavin sat pale and meek as a lamb for a few moments before going out to get Sandra for her interview.

Sandra wafted through like an ethereal being, she wasn't in her elf costume but some sort of flowy blouse and scarf number. Her hair was in a neat bun and she looked flushed, with nerves or excitement Ellie couldn't tell. She had seen the look on countless women from her childhood. It was the look of someone bursting to dish gossip as soon as they left.

"Good afternoon Ms Cullen, please take a seat." Ellie started formally. Sandra sat quickly as waited for further instruction.

"Now as you are aware we are investigating the death of Ron, it is looking like accidental death but we like to be thorough."

"Oh yes of course, such a shock too. Dear Ron was the life blood of this place, it won't be the same without him." She said with a solemn face.

"Well that's interesting that you would say that…we have heard from others that you didn't particularly like Ron, that in fact you were complaining about him only yesterday." Ellie said, watching carefully for the reaction.

Sandra flushed a darker red and moved uncomfortably in her seat.

"Well…ahem…yes…I may have had a few gripes but who doesn't when you work with someone? I bet she gets on your last nerve eh son?" Sandra implored Gavin who looked stonily back at her.

"Look Ron, when he was Santa, wouldn't mix or talk to us elves. The only person he would associate with was Mrs Claus…it was so stuck up and it got on my wick ok. But that doesn't mean I'm happy that the auld bugger is dead am I?" she admitted.

"Well now that's better, I don't need platitudes about the deceased, I need facts. So I'll ask for another, where were you last night after you finished here Sandra?"

"Oh you mean like an alibi?" Sandra was nearly beside herself with excitement.

"Oh now what did I do…um I walked home, it's not far, and then I made my dinner and watched the telly."

"Can anyone confirm that?"

"Well…no…I live alone, my son lives abroad now. Oh wait, my neighbour will have seen me come home, she's a nosey old cow and nothing happens in that street that she doesn't see."

"Ok, we may need to talk to her if this turns out to be anything other than an accident."

"Of course, not a problem." Sandra said with a smile. Ellie knew she was going to love passing this story on to her pals at the bingo.

Chapter 14

Kate was enjoying some rare peaceful hours at home while Aggie and Peggy were out doing the big shop. She was lying on the couch with a dog lying on each side of her. She had found the Vicar of Dibley Christmas special being repeated as she flicked through channels and settled down for some much needed rest. Her blissful idyll was shattered by Aggie rushing through the door.

"Oh Katie give me a hand, our Peggy's took a tumble!" she cried as she ran back out the door with Kate scrambling to her feet. Kate reached them as Aggie aided a hobbling Peggy through the front door and into the living room.

"What happened?" Kate asked in alarm as she wrapped an arm around Peggy's waist and guided her over to a chair. She then ran back outside for the shopping bags and dumped them in the kitchen before anyone could answer.

"Oh that little boy down the road threw a snowball at her, it hit her in the face and she slipped and went crashing down off the kerb." Aggie explained as Peggy growled her displeasure.

"Marcus...that wee swine I'll get him for this" Peggy threatened as she winced when her leg was raised on a cushion.

"Peggy he was just getting you back for that water trick!" Kate exclaimed.

"What water trick?" Aggie asked warily.

"Peggy made sure the pavement outside was like a sheet of ice and wee Marcus fell on it as he ran past." Kate explained.

"Margaret! He is a CHILD!" Aggie roared as she hit Peggy in the arm repeatedly with her handbag.

"He's not a child he's a little psychopath and I'll have him, you mark my words." muttered Peggy darkly as she watched him out the window. Marcus was celebrating his victory by running up and down outside and providing an impressive array of offensive hand gestures in Peggy's direction.

"Oh yes you laugh it up...you may have won the battle but not the war..."

Kate decided to change the subject as Peggy continued uttering curses of doom under her breath.

"Did you get the sprouts and the stuffing mum?"

"Aye we did, had to fight an old man for the last box of after eights mind you but we got everything we needed." Aggie said, her temper calming as she sat down.

"So who are we having for Christmas?" Kate asked as she went to make a cup of tea for everyone.

"Oh Seb and Rachel called to say they won't be coming. Their new business has really took off so they need to stay and cover the Christmas rush, they want to make sure there's a safe space open over the holiday period for anyone who needs it." Aggie said proudly.

"Good on them, so it's just us lot and Bill and Ann then?"

Kate confirmed as she put the shopping away.

"Aye, oh when is it they arrive?" Aggie asked.

"They're coming over on the 22nd, Ann is going spare because Bill hasn't started his shopping yet let alone packing." Kate said with a laugh. "She's dragging him up to Belfast to shop tomorrow."

"Any word from Ellie?" Aggie asked.

"Not yet, had a text to say she's doing interviews but nothing since." Kate responded.

"It's a shame all this has happened at Christmas. Oh did you get her present back in time?"

"Yeah it came today, I wrapped it while you were out. I hope she likes it." Kate said smiling.

"Oi, is there a tea going for the invalid in here?!" bellowed Peggy.

"You're not an invalid! You're a daft old woman fighting with a six year old!" Kate yelled back.

Chapter 15

"Why is this day never ending?" whined Gavin as they waited on their next interviewee.

"Steady big guy, you're just hungry. We'll send out for something after this next one. Who is it by the way?" Ellie asked.

"I dunno, a new guy is all I've been told."

Further conversation was not needed as they were interrupted by a large laugh.

"Aaaah no way man it's Batman and Robin! How you's doin eh?"

"Mark! What are you doing here?" Ellie asked as she got up to hug him. Mark was an ex youth offender that was now on the straight and narrow.

"I'm an elf! See Mrs Batman's maw asked me if I wanted to do it." Mark explained. It took Ellie a moment to realise he meant Aggie.

"Aye I thought it was a great idea man, give back to the local weans and that. So here I am, snazzy new outfit wi bells on! Ahahahaha" he laughed as he shook his foot up and down to make the bells jingle.

"That's great Mark, I'm proud of you." Ellie said earnestly and Mark blushed but was pleased.

"How come we haven't seen you before though? We've been in and out this week." Gavin asked as he pulled Mark in for a bear hug.

"I'm only here part time, I've still got to work see. I wasn't here yesterday cos I do my shift at the club. I'm the bar manager now" he said with pride, he stood a little taller.

"No way, that's great Mark, you're going up in the world." Ellie joked.

"Aye I am, my mums all chuffed too. I'm earning no a bad wage now you see, I pay her decent dig money and guess what I've got her for her Christmas? I've got her a cruise! She's always wanted to go on one, all-inclusive wine and all that. I saved up all year and finally was able to pay for it. She's gonna be buzzin, I canny wait until she opens that present." Mark beamed with pure happiness and Ellie couldn't be more pleased for him.

"How is your mum by the way?" Gavin asked.

"Aye she's great, I'm taking her up to the hospital this afternoon with her legs but she's fighting fit. She was round all the neighbours last night dishing out the cards and some shortbread for the older ones."

"Good on her, I'm glad she's doing well, send her our best wishes eh?"

"I will. Now what is it you need to ask me? Has he been done in or what?" Mark asked.

"Probably not but we need to cover our bases, if you weren't here yesterday then we don't really need to ask your whereabouts but you've already said you were at the club anyway. What I will ask is, what's your opinion on the other volunteers?" Ellie asked.

"To be honest, I don't really know any of them, except for Batman-mother-in-law that is. They seem to all stick together though, don't think they particularly like me but I'm no bothered. Old women either love me or think I'm gonna mug them and this lot are definitely of the mugger group so I try not to crowd them too much. Well if that's all, I need to get back to mum, if she doesn't get the early bus to the hospital she gets all stressed and then she ends up threatening the driver. You have a good Christmas eh?" Mark said as he hugged them both in turn once more before leaving the room.

Chapter 16

Gavin was more cheerful after he had been provided with a Greggs steak bake and a ham baguette. He was happily enjoying a post-lunch cup of tea before the next interview and had almost regained his usual charm before the arrival of the final interviewee.

"Oh by the way your Mhairi messaged me while you were away getting the lunch." Ellie said as she finished off her sausage roll. "She wants to know if you will be back at a reasonable hour tonight to carry on building the twins presents."

"It is honestly the one and only time that I will ever be buying stuff that needs built. Honestly Els, flatpack furniture with no instructions is easier to put together than the wee trike thing she's bought."

"Do you need a hand with it?" Ellie asked as she tipped a generous amount of sugar into her own tea.

"Nah, I'm dad so I should build their stuff. I mean, the trike might just be a one off and the rest of the gear will be easy enough to put together. I'll have a good go at it tonight and I'm sure it will be fine." Gavin said with confidence that neither of them felt.

The last of the volunteer elves announced her arrival with a feral sounding growl coming from behind Gavin.

"Oooh if you are what counts as police these days then I should get myself arrested once in a while" she purred as she slinked her way over and sat on the desk in front of Gavin. This woman had the attitude of Mae West but the body of Norah Batty, the desk creaked under her weight as she crossed her legs in what she hoped was a Sharon Stone-esque manner. Gavin had gone quite pale and Ellie cleared her throat to catch the woman's attention but she may as well have been a piece of furniture for all the attention she was paid.

"Can you please sit on the chair provided and we can start this interview?" Ellie said with a hint of coolness in her voice, she had already lost patience with this one as she attempted to run her elf boot up Gavin's leg. The woman finally acquiesced to the demand and sat in the chair but she kept her eyes on Gavin.

"Your name please" Ellie said loudly.

Vikki Bannerman…single…" she said to Gavin.

"And can you tell me your thoughts on the man that played Santa, Ron?" Ellie persevered.

"Oh…I'm not keen on him to be honest…dull little man. I mean here I am looking like I do, and all he talked about was his garden and his allotment. All of this beauty and womanhood wasted on a man like that." She whispered as she leant forward to try to touch Gavin's leg but he shot back so fast he nearly cannonballed himself through the wall.

"Ms Bannerman…why did you volunteer for this festive

grotto?" it wasn't an investigative question but Ellie was at a loss as to why this woman who acted and dressed like a character from 'On the buses' would be volunteering for a children's charity.

"Oh well...I thought I would meet some eligible single fathers by doing this, I mean it's just the type of thing they would do with their weekend access isn't it. But not a sniff so far." She said with a depression that was reserved for a southern Belle when her beau went off to war. Ellie had heard enough and wanted her out.

"Ms Bannerman where were you after you finished here yesterday?"

"Well after I left here I met my very good friend Viola for a festive refreshment and then went home."

"Alone?"

"Sadly yes...but if this one isn't busy, I'm hoping to reverse that luck tonight." She purred as she practically lunged for Gavin, whose reflexes served him well once more as he dodged out of her clutches.

"I can assure you he is busy and if you don't stop that I'll do you for sexual harassment" Ellie threatened as she stood to her full height.

Vikki considered her for a moment before sighing and waddling out of the room.

"Thanks Els..." Gavin said quietly as he sat back down.

"She needs a therapist." Ellie muttered.

"Therapist? She needs a truck load of medication and a strait jacket!" Gavin said with a whimper.

Chapter 17

Ellie arrived at the office shaking snow off her coat, Gavin walked slowly behind her still in shock and sat down without a word.

"What's up with him?" Kent asked as she set some files on Ellie's desk.

"He's just went ten rounds with Ursula from the Little Mermaid. He'll be alright after he's had some time and a bit of counselling. Anything come in for us while we've been out?"

"Yes ma'am, Doc Brett has sent over her report on the post-mortem." Kent responded as she watched Simpson hand Gavin a cup of tea and pat his shoulder sympathetically.

"Doc says that she has changed her original cause of death from accidental death to murder."

"Sorry what?" Ellie asked in shock. Kent even had to re-read what she had just said.

"Sorry ma'am I hadn't looked over this until now…but yes Doc says murder. Um…according to her report, death was caused by repeated blunt force trauma to the skull. The pattern of injury does not make sense for a fall from height. She has also made note to check the forensic report ma'am."

Kent finished as she flicked through several other reports. "Ah ok, forensics tested many items located around the scene and found blood on one item in particular, Santa's bell that was found beside the body was dented and covered in the victim's blood…no prints on the handle."

"Ok…so we now have a crime scene and a murder weapon. I'm glad we spent the day interviewing the volunteers, it means we have a head start in trying to piece together who would have wanted to kill Santa." Ellie said with a sigh as she stood and walked towards the murder board.

"So every person who was with Ron last night has provided us with their whereabouts once they left. The problem is…there is a chance someone killed him before they left but I don't think they would have had time to stage the scene. Simpson can you pull CCTV from the area around the community centre? I think the wee shop across the road has a camera outside. I want to know if everyone left when they said they did. None of them have cast iron alibis except Aggie, Peggy and possibly Mark if we can confirm that he was working his shift at the club. All the others can't corroborate their alibis as they were alone for the most part. Kent I want you to dig in to Ron's life, see if he owed money or had any issues or if he was a secret drug dealer or…I don't know…anything in his life worth killing him for…also check this lot's phone records to see if any of them had regular contact with Ron, from what they've said none of them were exactly best pals with him so it would be unusual enough for us to be interested. I want this solved quickly ladies and…well…Gavin… I want us all to be able to relax and enjoy Christmas as soon as possible. Now go home and we start fresh in the morning, night everyone."

Chapter 18

Ellie arrived home quicker than she thought, the snow had kept a lot of the more cautious drivers off the roads so she made her way home on empty roads for once. Peggy was snoozing in a chair by the fire, her leg up on a stool and Bruiser lying beside her, legs in the air and snoring loudly, although so was Peggy.

"Hi honey, how was work?" Kate asked quietly as she got up from the couch to welcome Ellie with a kiss and a hug.

"Well we are now dealing with a murder, not an accident and Gavin has been traumatised by an aging femme fatale." Ellie responded and then explained the interviews and Doc's post-mortem results.

"Poor Ron, he always seemed like such a nice man, I can't think of someone wanting to kill him." Kate mused as she set a bowl of stew that Aggie had made earlier in front of Ellie who attacked the meal with enthusiasm.

"Well someone had issue with him…not many of the volunteers appeared to like him very much but it's still early days…hopefully something will come to light. How was your choir practice this morning?"

"It went really well, we sound good considering as individuals half of us sound like cats in heat. We're all set for the performance tomorrow with mums grotto people." Kate said confidently.

"Are they still going ahead? How can they without a Santa?" Ellie asked in confusion.

"They've picked another Santa…" Kate hesitated. "Peggy is the new Santa."

"Oh good god how did that happen?" Ellie asked in shock.

"No one else wanted the gig basically. She won't be able to get into much trouble anyway, she's hurt her leg falling on ice today so she'll be sitting down for the majority of the time."

"She fell? Is she ok?" Ellie asked with concern.

"Oh aye she's fine, don't feel sorry for the old rogue she got what she deserved." Kate muttered but Ellie looked at her for further explanation.

"She iced the pavement to make sure that Marcus slipped as he was running around, he got his revenge by belting her with a snowball and causing her to slip in the same spot."

"Oh god she's still fighting with that wean across the street? What is he like seven?" Ellie moaned.

"He's six and yes she's in full military mode with this vendetta, she's planning something." Kate said just as Peggy's phone rang. She jolted awake and answered the call furtively.

"Hello…yes I'm glad you called me back Fergie…I need you to do me a wee favour on the quiet…no nothing too big… but I think it will be effective…" she spoke quietly as she hobbled past them and out to the garden.

"Isn't Fergie one of her not-so-legal hackers?" Ellie asked

as she watched Peggy hobble around the garden talking animatedly.

"He is...I thought getting her to volunteer would keep her out of trouble" Kate groaned.

Chapter 19

The next morning they were all assembled at St Enoch's shopping centre. The decorations were beautiful, they had pulled out all the stops to have Santa's grotto and fake snow, a real reindeer and a stage set up for the choir. There was a large crowd waiting for the performance as it was a celebrity choir, the tv crews were there to get the feelgood segment for the news at six. Peggy had walked out gingerly with the aid of a walking stick, dressed in the full Santa suit and bellowing deep "Ho Ho Ho's". The children cheered as she waved to them, she tried to hug Mrs Claus but accidentally trod on Aggie's foot as she did so and got rewarded with a sharp elbow to the ribs. They sit down as the choir takes their place and starts with a rendition of 'O little town of Bethlehem' as the charity buckets started to be passed around the audience by more volunteers dressed as reindeer and snowmen.

Times are hard for everyone right now but Ellie watched as people were digging deep to fill the buckets. It was a charity for underprivileged children and their families. Glaswegians may be gruff at times but they will do anything for the weans, especially at Christmas. Ellie watched all this with a smile, it always made her love her adopted city more. She watched as the kids in the audience waved at Santa and sang along with the choir.

She turned back to watching the choir and in particular, she watched Kate as she stood in the front row singing with the sopranos of the group.

Ellie was lost watching and listening for a long time until a scream snapped her to attention. She turned to see a speaker plummeting down and crashing on to the chair that Peggy had been sitting on but had managed to fling herself out of with remarkable speed before it hit. Ellie ran forward as the crowd watched on in horror. Kate was at Ellie's heels as she reached Aggie and Peggy.

"Are you ok?" she asked breathlessly as she helped Aggie up who had also dived off her seat. Peggy got up a little gingerly and hobbled on her bad leg towards a chair that had been brought forward by the choir members.

"We're fine, bruised from landing but I've got enough padding. Where the bloody hell did that speaker come from?" Peggy asked with a grimace as she sat down and then looked up towards the upper floors where the speakers for the choir's microphones had been rigged.

Ellie was also looking but with a sense of dread and fear. Her worry was that someone had murderous intent not towards Ron, but towards Santa and Peggy had narrowly escaped a possible murder attempt.

<h1 style="text-align:center">Chapter 20</h1>

The area is cleared by local PCs except those who had been filming the incident. The news crews had shown their footage and a handful of people had gathered round Ellie and were dutifully handing over their phones for her to watch the footage. Gavin walked over as she was studying two phones intently. He had been helping Peggy over to get checked by some paramedics.

"How's Peggy?" she asked without looking up.

"Oh, she's having a great time! They've got her on some painkillers, and she's went giddy! I left her as she was telling the ambulance crew how much she loved them and invited them round for Hogmanay."

Ellie nodded, her focus still on the videos in front of her.

"Got anything?" he asked quietly to avoid alerting the nine sets of ears currently trying to eavesdrop while waiting for their phones back.

"Not really...none of the videos show the moment the speaker was detached from its position; they're all trained on the choir or on the grotto." Ellie murmured.

"So, nothing then." Gavin sighed.

"Not quite...I've noticed something important being

missing for several minutes before the crash."

"What?" Gavin asked as he peered over her shoulder at the video, but he couldn't see what she meant.

"None of Santa's elves are anywhere in this footage, they were supposed to be hanging around the grotto...so where are they all?"

She was right, Gavin went through all the footage too at her request to make sure she wasn't missing them in obvious places but not one of them featured as soon as the choir started singing.

"Get them over here and we'll get their alibis for this, I'm not having this violence last another day!" Ellie was angry that her family had, once again, been placed in danger, and all they had done was volunteer their time for charity.

"I'll round them up" Gavin said quietly as he gripped her shoulder. There was no need though, Kent had been keeping them with her, just in case, and Gavin was able to bring them forward individually to be interviewed. First up was Robbie.

"Is that woman alright? The shouty one that plays Santa? Honestly this grotto is cursed!" Robbie started but Ellie was in no mood.

"Robbie you and the other elves were supposed to be milling around when the choir was performing so that you could hand out sweets and take donations. None of you were present, where were you?" Ellie asked bluntly. Robbie looked a little startled, but he composed himself very quickly.

"Well...um...oh I was inside the grotto. I was tidying up and sorting out the candy canes to give out after the choir performance. I thought there were enough people out amongst the crowd so I would do something productive with the time." He shrugged.

"Did you tell anyone what you were doing?" Gavin asked.

"Well, no…it was a spur of the moment thing…thought it would help Aggie when she was handing out the canes to have them all organised in bundles." He explained with a further shrug.

"Thank you, Robbie, that's all for now, can you send the next person over when you leave, please?" Ellie responded. Robbie took the dismissal well and nodded as he left.

"Els you need to calm down and keep your head, I know you're angry, I am too but we need to get information from this lot, and it will be easier done if they are at ease." Gavin muttered. Ellie sighed and nodded her head.

Thankfully the next person to be interviewed was Mark. He didn't arrive with his usual laugh and cheerful banter though, he was pale and looked on the verge of tears.

"You ok Mark?" Ellie asked, her mood from moments ago replaced with concern.

"Aye…just canny believe that big Peggy was nearly killed and that your maw-in-law was close to it too…they're nice ladies who don't deserve that." He said quietly. Ellie grasped his hand and squeezed it gently, smiling at thoughtful face.

"They're ok Mark, I imagine by now that Peggy will be trying to dance with the tallest paramedic and…probably singing a dirty limerick at him. Did you see what happened?"

"No, I was standing beside Mrs Batman in the choir. I was singing along to the songs you see, I used to love singing them at school…one of the few things I turned up for…and she heard me and dragged me up beside her to sing…she's very kind is your missus…" he said with a blush.

"That she is" Ellie said with a grin, once he said about the singing, she remembered hearing a loud baritone in the middle of the sopranos. She grabbed one of the phones and played the footage of the choir and yes, she had missed him, Mark was standing arm in arm with Kate as they belted out a rendition of 'away in a manger'.

"Did you see any of the other volunteers from where you were standing?"

"No, I don't think so…I wasn't really paying attention though…was enjoying mysel too much." Mark said with a smile.

"Fair enough, Mark do us a favour and hang around until we've finished. I might have a wee job for you." Ellie said.

"No bother at all Batman, you only have tae ask." Mark said brightly, his face now clear of the tears from minutes before.

"Good lad, send the next one over when you head back, and don't tell any of them that you know us ok?"

"Will do" he said with a little salute as he left.

Annie came forward next, but she surprised them all by dragging Sandra along with her.

"I hear you're wanting our alibis; I must say I don't like being treated like some common criminal, not like that dodgy looking wee bloke that you just interviewed…he's got evil eyes him…well me and Sandra here went out for a sly smoke while that tone deaf lot were singing." Annie said defiantly before Ellie or Gavin had got a word in. Sandra looked startled for a moment but then composed herself and nodded her agreement.

"I see, and did either of you happen to witness the events?" Ellie asked.

"No, as I said, we were both out the side doors smoking." Annie said with finality before she turned on her heels and marched off, still dragging Sandra along in her wake.

"Well, that's us told, eh?" Gavin muttered as he watched her retreating form.

"Hmmm, Sandra didn't look too comfortable, did she? She never opened her mouth once." Ellie mused.

"She never got a chance, hell we barely got a chance!" Gavin said as they watched Vikki start to ooze in their direction.

"Oh god here she comes again, Els you deal with her I'm still not recovered from the last time." Gavin said in panic as he stood behind Ellie for protection.

"We meet again" Vikki purred as she stood in front of Ellie but peered around her towards the cowering hulk of fear behind her. "Oh, are you acting all shy today…I love that in a man" she continued as she tried to dart past Ellie, but she wasn't quick enough.

"Vikki, can you focus on me long enough to answer a question? Where were you during the choir performance?" Ellie asked as she kept her movement swift to head off Vikki's further advancement toward Gavin.

"Well…now I don't want to make you jealous my love, but I have another suitor and I was with him during the carol service thing. He's a security guard here and I spent the time in his wee office down there" she hitched her thumb behind to towards a side door that was clearly marked

'Security'

"Of course, I will stop all fraternisation with him at once if you only say the word" she whispered towards Gavin. "I'll let you see my Christmas stocking" she added and that was enough to make even Ellie queasy.

"Thank you, Vikki, that will be all for now. We will of course need to verify your story with the man in question.

"Of course, darling, his name is Mike, ask him and he'll tell you E-ver-y-thing" she blew a kiss at Gavin and flounced off.

"Never leave me alone with her Els...promise me" Gavin begged as he sighed in relief that the ordeal was over for now.

Chapter 21

Ellie pulls Aggie, Peggy, and Mark into the grotto for an emergency meeting.

"Are the other volunteers still here?" Ellie asked as she closed the door behind her.

"I think so, they're sat in Starbucks having a coffee at the moment." Aggie responded.

"Ok, I want you all to be my eyes and ears. I need you to try and either break their alibis or confirm them. Now Annie says she and Sandra were out smoking, Robbie says he was in here sorting out candy canes and Vikki was chatting up some poor beggar in security. Now Gavin is on his way to speak to the security guard, Mark can you try to chat to Annie or Sandra and see what you can find out? Aggie you take Robbie, see what you can find out about him being here and Peggy…" Ellie stopped as she noticed that Peggy was fast asleep in a chair, the painkillers had properly kicked in by now. "Marvellous." Ellie muttered as she opened the door and beckoned for a nearby PC. "Can you get her home safely?" she asked quietly, and he nodded as he stepped forward and, with strength he didn't look capable of, hoisted Peggy over his shoulder in a fireman's lift. The last thing they say was Peggy waking up long enough to shout, "Hi Ho Silver, away!" and then slumped over again before she was carried out the side door.

"What will you be doing Ellie?" Aggie asked as she worried about that poor man's back after lifting Peggy.

"I'm going to go look at the fixtures of the speaker, I'm taking someone from forensics with me, I need to see how it was tampered with. There's no way this was accidental. Catch me up later if you find anything." They both nodded their understanding and left the room, and then Aggie came back in as she remembered this was where Robbie was supposed to be.

"Daft auld bugger" she muttered to herself as she started to snoop around the room.

Gavin walked into the security office to find a young man breathing into a paper bag and being patted on the back by an older man, both in security uniform.

"I'm looking for Mike?" Gavin asked.

"That's him there, but give him a minute, he's had a hell of a shock." Explained the older man as he looked at Mike kindly, his name badge said 'Reg'. "Some woman; old enough to be his gran tried it on with him and gave him the fright of his life. If I hadn't walked in when I did God knows what would have happened to the poor lad." He whispered as Mike continued to hyperventilate into the bag, his hands shaking as he held it over his face.

"It was horrible…she just lunged at me…it was like fighting off a giant squid" Mike shuddered as he repressed the memory.

"Here son, just keep breathing into this, Ivy is coming with a cup of tea for you, that'll sort you out." Reg said as he continued to pat his shoulder in a fatherly manner.

"When did this woman leave?" Gavin asked.

"I bundled her out when I heard the screaming out on the ground floor, she wasn't for budging up until then. She needs looking at does that one!" Reg said with feeling.

"You're not wrong" muttered Gavin as a look of understanding passed between himself and Mike. "You'll be ok soon, just avoid her as best you can, she'll be out of here soon."

"I'm not shifting out of here until she goes, and my mum is coming to make sure I get home unmolested." Mike explained shakily. Gavin left knowing that Vikki did have an alibi but feeling sorry for the poor boy left traumatised in the room behind him.

Aggie was poking around in the Grotto, not really sure what she was looking for, Robbie was up in Starbucks with the others, but she didn't think talking to him would get her anywhere. She was going through the storage boxes that they had brought from the community centre when it suddenly struck her, they hadn't brought candy canes with them! There was no room in the car once all the other stuff was packed so they decided to leave them.

"Oh Robbie you little liar." she whispered to herself as she closed the boxes and made her way out of the grotto.

Mark was hanging around opposite Starbucks watching Annie and Sandra. Annie was chatting animatedly to Vikki, but Sandra was just stirring her coffee absently. When the ladies got up to leave, he sneaked ahead of them and stood just outside the front doors. It wasn't long before they made their way outside, still chatting. Mark made his move.

"Hiya ladies, that you heading up the road then?" he asked

cheerfully as he lit a cigarette. "Oh, where are my manners, would any of you like one?" he asked as he proffered the packet to them. Vikki declined with a smile, Annie said no she's heading for the subway and needed to rush, and Sandra pointedly turned her nose up at the offer with a prim "No thank you, disgusting habit" before marching out onto Buchanan Street and away.

"Yeah, that's what I thought" muttered Mark. When Ellie had explained the alibi Mark remembered the fuss Sandra had made when there was a mix-up with their costumes, and she got his elf tunic by mistake. She went mental because it smelled of smoke and how it got into her hair. There's no way she was out having a sly smoke today. "I could be good at this polis thing" he thought to himself as he flicked the cigarette butt out into the street. He was then accosted by the shopping centre's cleaner.

"Oi, get that picked up or I'll make you eat it!" she bellowed at him. He sheepishly picked it up and put it in the bin. "Sorry missus" he muttered before scrambling away.

<h1 style="text-align:center">Chapter 22</h1>

Ellie comes home after waiting on forensics to test the speaker and its fixtures. They found no prints but did find confirmation that it had been no accident. The rope holding the speaker in place had been cut through.

As Ellie came through the door she was met with Aggie, Kate, a now conscious Peggy and Mark.

"How did it go Ellie?" Peggy asked, more alert than she's been for hours. "The others have been filling me in." she explained.

"The speaker was tampered with, cut down in fact. But we found no prints on anything." Ellie explained as she shrugged off her coat and kissed Kate hello.

"Well, if you're thinking it was one of the elves, there wouldn't be any prints." said Peggy. "They all wear gloves." she said as Ellie looked confused.

"Terrific" she muttered as she sat down with a sigh. "Did anyone else find out anything useful?"

"We did." said Aggie excitedly "You first Mark love"

"Aw thanks, well I waited on old Annie and Sandra outside, and I offered them each a cigarette. Sandra turned her nose up at it completely, told me it was a filthy habit. It reminded me that she had complained about her costume stinking of smoke when hers got mixed with mine. So that's a lie then, isn't it?" he asked, pleased with his investigations.

"It is, although Sandra wasn't the one that said it, but she didn't deny it either." Ellie mused.

"It means I doubt either of their alibis are true, and here's another one for you. Robbie couldn't have been organising candy canes as we never brought any." Aggie added triumphantly. "So he's not got an alibi either."

"That leaves Vikki left to be accounted for, I've left a message for Gav to call me, Mhairi has him building toys tonight."

As she said that, the doorbell rang. Kate got up to answer and was met with Gavin almost in tears as he holds up trike pieces.

"Els I can't...it doesn't make sense...the bloody thing doesn't fit together." He wailed as he sat on the living room floor looking despondent. Mark took pity on him and sat down to help.

"Leave it to me, I was forever building things like this for my cousins." He said as he got to work. Gavin scrambled up to go to his car and came back with boxes full of toys that needed assembly. He kissed Mark's head in complete gratitude as he slumped into a chair looking exhausted.

"Don't judge me Ellie" he muttered as she had her 'told you so' face on. "Mark, I'll see you right if you can get this lot fixed up."

"Nah this one's on the house, can't have those weans playing with dangerous toys can I" Mark joked as he worked away and had the trike fixed up in minutes. He moved on to one of the other toys.

"Gav, did you visit with security?" Ellie asked.

"Aye, Vikki was there alright, she turned her charm on a lad of twenty and scared the hell out of him. She was in there leching on the poor soul until the speaker came down." He responded as he watched Mark with fascination.

"Well, it appears that the only alibi that stood up was Vikki's, we'll need to pull the others back in tomorrow and get some answers. What was Robbie really doing? If Annie was indeed having a smoke, why did she lie about Sandra doing the same? And why did Sandra go along with it?" Ellie thought out loud. Her musings were broken by the arrival of Bill and Ann, they bustled through the door laden with gift bags and suitcases.

"You made it safe then?" Kate said as she hugged Ann and helped her with bags.

"Aye only just, I thought getting the ferry would be less stressful, but I wasn't banking on bloody Stirling Moss here flying down that A77 like a man possessed!" she grumbled as Bill smiled sheepishly.

"Got a new car Ellie love, Audi R8, V10 engine oh you should hear it when you open it up on a clear road." Bill said blissfully.

"Humph, it's noisy, has bugger all boot space and the back seats are non-existent." Ann retaliated.

"Ach who needs backseats" Bill waived her aside as he hugged everyone.

"Where are we putting presents then? Under the tree?" he asked as he started to haul brightly wrapped gifts out of bags and placed them under the tree.

Ellie watched on as her family (adopted and born) chatted, laughed and in Peggy, Aggie, and Ann's case, drank. Bill dropped to the floor to help Mark with the toys and Gavin helped Kate to take the dogs for a walk.

'This is all I need for Christmas' Ellie thought happily before rolling her eyes at her own soppiness.

Chapter 23

Ellie and Gavin are watching through the two way mirror as the first of their suspects sat nervously picking apart a tissue. Sandra looked pale as she sat at the table, she had refused legal counsel claiming she had nothing to hide. They walked through the door and sat opposite her. Gavin started the tape.

"This interview is taking place on 23rd December at 9.16am. In attendance is DI Bickerton and Detective Superintendent McVey." Gavin said for the tape.

"Now Sandra, when we asked for your whereabouts yesterday during the incident with the speaker that nearly caused the death of one of your volunteers. We now have further evidence that this was not an accident but in fact a serious attempt at harm or murder." Ellie let that bit sink in before she continued. Sandra hadn't looked away from her once, she was transfixed.

"So Sandra, you can see why we are a bit concerned when we realised that your alibi was a fabrication. You weren't out smoking, in fact you abhor smoking we have been told…so would you care to explain?"

"I…um…oh what's the point." Sandra sighed. "Annie asked if I would cover for her. She must have her reasons of course, but it put me in a bit of a spot."

"Did she tell you why she wanted you to lie?" Ellie asked.

"No, just that she had a really good reason and she would explain later, but she never did."

"I see, so where were you yesterday if you weren't outside smoking?"

"I was in the loo if you must know…I've had a weak bladder since I hit 60 and I need to go more often…and those elf tights are a bugger to get down when you're in a hurry. It wouldn't be the first time that I had been caught short and I wasn't taking any chances." Sandra said as she crossed her arms as if to end this particular interview.

"Thank you, we'll check your alibi of course, and if you can think of anything to help, just let us know." Ellie said.

"Y…yes of course, anything I can do…and I'm sorry for not speaking up…I thought I was helping a friend. I didn't know that it was a serious matter, if I'd known it was attempted murder then I would have spoken up before." She said, her face full of shame.

As Gavin showed Sandra out, he came back with Annie who had been drinking copious amounts of tea in reception and was now a bit jittery. As they sat down Gavin repeated the information for the tape as he had done with Sandra's interview. Annie had also opted for no legal counsel.

"Annie we have a few questions regarding your alibi for yesterday…first I would like you to know that we are treating the incident as attempted murder and are taking this investigation seriously. With that in mind, can you tell us why you lied about who you were with?" Ellie asked, no point in beating about the bush she thought.

"What do you mean?" she answered guardedly.

"I mean that Sandra wasn't with you, she's confirmed that to us just now. So why did you say she was?"

"It's…well…oh God it's so embarrassing…my ex man was in the audience yesterday, I clocked him when I was handing out some sweets. He was with his new bit of stuff, what's her name…Amanda…and well…I mean I looked like a bag of washing didn't I… a festive bag albeit but a bag nonetheless. I couldn't let him see me dressed like a bloody Snowman could I? So I hid…I hid in the grotto until the speaker crashed and everything went mad. I slipped back out during the chaos and he never spotted me." Annie admitted.

"Why didn't you just say that?" Ellie asked.

"Because it's pathetic, a grown woman hiding in a glorified shed from her ex and his tart. I didn't want people to know…so I lied, made up a wee tale about smoking and thought it would sound better if someone was with me so I said Sandra…she's a pal and I knew she would back me up if I asked. I'm sorry I messed you about hen…I should have just been honest."

"Thank you for being honest now…hang on…you said you hid in the grotto?"

"Yes, it was the closest place I could hide in."

"Was there anyone else in there?" Ellie asked, hoping it would solidify a point for the next suspect.

"Well no, I was in there myself." Annie said with a confused frown.

"You're certain no one else entered the grotto in the time that you were there?"

"Well I think I would have bloody noticed hen, it's hardly a life sized model of Buckingham Palace is it?"

"Yes…good point…well I think that's all we need to know for now, we'll be in touch." Ellie said bringing the interview to a close.

Annie left and Gavin turned round to whisper to her. "Proof that Robbie wasn't in the grotto…nice one!"

"Yeah I liked that little bit too…bring him in and we'll see what he has to say for himself."

Robbie was led in and sat down, he was sweating profusely and his leg was jiggling up and down so much it shook his cup of water on the table over. Once again Gavin went through the information for the tape.

"So Robbie, new information has come to light that puts your alibi in question. First of all you told us that you were in the grotto sorting out candy canes. We now know that the grotto event never brought candy canes with them yesterday, something to do with car storage. We also have a witness that testified that you were not in the grotto at any point in the moments before the incident. So would you like to correct your previous statement and give a true account of what you were doing yesterday?" Ellie said. Robbie had gone grey by this point, sweat beading on his forehead and soaking through his t-shirt.

"I wasn't entirely honest with you about my army days. I served don't get me wrong, but I um…I got diagnosed with PTSD after my last tour in Kabul and was medically discharged. I'm on a pension but it's not a great amount… everything is going up in price and I've got to pay child support or else I wouldn't see my weans. I'm in serious debt now and I need money to put the leccy on and get my kids some presents for Christmas…I'm allowed them for a bit on Christmas day so long as the flat is warm." Robbie took a shaky breath before continuing. "I was desperate… what I was doing when the speaker crashed was…well I was nicking folks wallets and purses…I needed cash…I'm so sorry" he started to sob, his entire body drained from the stress.

"I um…I still have a couple of them…I'll return them obviously and I understand what needs to happen now." He said with finality.

"I'm sorry Robbie…I am arresting you on suspicion of theft you do not have to say anything but anything you do say will be used in evidence." Ellie recited to him as he nodded, tears falling down his cheeks. Ellie felt horrible, she hoped that the courts would take pity on him.

Chapter 24

Ellie and Gavin sat down at their desks after their interviews, the last one didn't sit well with Ellie, she didn't want to have to charge a desperate man just before Christmas. Gavin's silence told her he felt the same.

"Simpson can you get on to security at the St Enoch Centre and ask them if they've had reports of stolen wallets or if they've found any? It would seem that Robbie Banks' alibi is that he was in the crowd nicking wallets. He also said he was discharged from the army so Kent can you get on to your contacts and see if that holds up?" Ellie said with a sigh.

"Why steal off folk at a charity event?" Simpson asked shaking her head.

"He was desperate, he wanted to make sure his house was warm and that he had presents so that he could see his kids. I'm not condoning what he did, but I doubt he will be the only one this Christmas." Gavin said quietly.

"As for the others, Sandra's new alibi is that she was in the bogs and Annie was hiding in the grotto so that her ex-man didn't see her. See if any of the video footage or CCTV shows either of these things." Ellie said.

Ellie stood up and walked to the murder board, something wasn't sitting right with her about this case.

"Kent do me a favour, run a background on our first victim Ron, I want to know if he's ever had so much as a parking ticket or any issues with the law, I want anything in his life that looks remotely dodgy. Is he a flasher by night? Is he an underground drug dealer for the local bingo? I want to know, because I'm not convinced that this is the work of some nutter who hates Santa. The attack on Peggy was too similar to the first incident with Ron, I think it was staged to throw us off track with this investigation."

"Why would someone do that?" Simpson asked.

"You kill one person then we look for motive and links, you kill a few people then we look for patterns in the kill as a serial killer has widely different psychopathy. Am I right Boss?" Gavin explained.

"Yup, gold star to you" Ellie quipped. "I'm not saying we don't look into Peggy's near escape, but I don't think she was honestly a target. I want reports by the morning people, it's nearly Christmas and I know you all have your plans so hopefully we'll all get some downtime, eh?"

A hopeful cheer followed this as the team set to work.

Chapter 25

Ellie arrived home to wonderful aromas coming from the kitchen. Aggie and Ann had joined forces to make a lovely dinner for them all. As Ellie followed her nose and stomach to the kitchen, she saw the two matriarchs of the family chatting happily as they stirred pots and bustled with plates. At their feet was Bella and Bruiser, on hand just in case anything happened to fall, and they would clear it up. Ann occasionally would drop a little bit of roast beef down for each of them and would set a duo of tails wagging happily at the stolen feast.

"She's blackmailing them because she's giving them a festive bath after dinner." Kate whispered in her ear as she kissed her.

"That will be fun for her, does she know it usually takes three people and a miracle to give Bella a bath without someone getting hurt?" Ellie whispered back as she brought Kate in for a hug that warmed her soul.

"Nah, leaving that as a nice wee surprise for her" Kate said with a chuckle.

"Dinner's ready, put each other down and get sat at the table" Ann instructed them as she set plates down that were piled high with roasted vegetables and potatoes.

"Ann, are you doing a trial run at Christmas dinner? This is massive!" Kate exclaimed.

"Just making sure your stomachs are all trained for a big feed" she joked as she set gravy down.

"Smells good in here" Peggy said as she walked in with Bill and sat down, immediately starting to dig in to her own massive plate.

"How's your leg now Peggy?" Ellie asked as she started to attack her plate with similar enthusiasm to Peggy and Bill.

"Aye it's not as bad, I can walk a bit better on it today, in fact Bill and I walked your two terrors in the park earlier."

As they were chatting about their day the doorbell rang, Ellie got up to answer it.

"Is that older woman in please?" asked the small voice at the door. Ellie didn't need to ask which one, she turned and walked back to the kitchen.

"Peggy, you've got a gentleman caller" she announced as she led Marcus into the kitchen, he looked defeated.

"What can I do for you young man?" Peggy asked in her no-nonsense manner.

"Truce" he mumbled holding out his hand. She considered him for a moment before smiling and shaking his hand.

"Truce agreed." She said simply.

"Can you put it all back now?" he asked quietly.

"I will, and that's the end of it yes?" Peggy said.

"Yes" he responded.

"OK, I'll sort that for you now, it should all be back when you get home."

"Thanks" and with that he left.

"Old woman what have you done?" Kate asked with her eyes narrowed.

"Moi? I did nothing, although I'm told that young Marcus' Minecraft account got hacked…all of his world that he had spent so much time building…it all disappeared to be replaced by one avatar that looked remarkably like me." Peggy said lightly as she filled her mouth with sprouts. She looked thoroughly pleased with herself.

"Are you trying to tell me that you got one of your hackers to hack a six-year-olds computer game?!" Aggie hissed.

"It worked, didn't it? He won't be a problem anymore." Peggy replied and Aggie could think of nothing to say to her but got up and brought the bottle of baileys over and poured herself and Ann a large glass each.

"I can't believe you did that" Kate sat stunned, her own fork frozen midway to her mouth.

"Ah what are you all worried about? It stopped the hostilities, didn't it? Do you know how many times I have used a similar ploy against certain countries over the years? A six year old is no different to some world leaders… I knew it would work" she said, satisfied that she had a Christmas Armistice in the snowball war of 2022.

Chapter 26

Santa's Grotto resumed at the community centre the next morning, it was Christmas Eve so people were swarming to the event as a nice festive treat for their kids. Aggie and Ann had finished the first bottle of baileys very quickly with dinner last night and decided to make some mulled wine as a night cap, they drank the entire pot and sat up to three in the morning cackling away and sharing horror stories of disastrous Christmases of their past. Aggie was regretting her life choices this morning as hundreds of screaming children were excitedly running around.

"Oh god I forgot how bloody loud weans are at Christmas" she croaked, her voice gone from too much talking and laughing.

"I have no sympathy for you Aggie dear" Peggy responded piously as, for once, she had gone to bed early and sober. Peggy was relishing her role of Santa this morning, her victory over Marcus had given her the Christmas cheer she had been missing. She was bellowing "Ho Ho Ho" at the top of her lungs so often that Aggie was contemplating hitting *her* with that bloody bell.

"Elves, send in the next child!" she shouted importantly, and it was Mark that was on line duty today so he grinned and brought forward the next kid. This was the one that finished Aggie off, her hangover could not take it. The kid obviously had a bit of a cold, he sat on Santa's knee, facing Mrs Claus, with an enormous snot bubble expanding in his left nostril. Aggie watched it expand and contract as the kid breathed in and out. She went pale the second it burst and excused herself very quickly as she ran to the bathroom.

"You see young Kenny, Mrs Claus had one too many mince pies last night so she's not feeling very well, but don't worry, I'm fighting fit and still able to deliver presents tonight. Now what would you like for Christmas young man?" Peggy said with mirth.

Peggy had given three more children some gifts after Kenny, before Aggie made a reappearance. She was shaky but looked like she had regained some colour to her face.

"Feeling better, are we?" Peggy chirped.

"Get stuffed Santa" she replied as she sat in her chair and drank from a bottle of water.

Peggy chuckled and called to Mark for the next child in the queue. Her mirth instantly stopped when Marcus came through and crawled up on her knee. Peggy sat in silence for a minute before getting a kick from Aggie.

"Oh…ahem…hello young man…and what can Santa do for you today? Have you been a good boy this year?" she asked gruffly in a deep voice. Marcus obviously didn't recognise her in the outfit, he sat staring down at the ground.

"No Santa, I've not been good. I'm sorry." He whispered.

"Well…what have you done, then I can assess if you've been good enough for a gift" another kick from Aggie.

"I've been hitting people with snowballs…I'm sorry and I won't do it again…" he said quietly and even Peggy warmed a little.

"Well…seeing as you're sorry…I think we can overlook that this year…so what do you want from Santa then?" Peggy said, a little more kindly, which gained an approving smile from Aggie.

"I want someone to play with" Marcus replied.

"Eh?" Peggy was thrown by this request.

"I've got toys Santa…but I don't have anyone to play with. I don't have any brothers or sisters and my mum is too busy. I used to play with my Gran…but she's had to move away… I don't get to see her much anymore…." Marcus tailed off, a little sniffle showing his emotion.

"I see, so you're lonely?" Peggy asked gently.

"Yeah…spose so." he said with a shrug, now embarrassed.

"Tell me, if you had someone to play with, what would you play?"

"Same things I used to play with Gran, hide and seek or soldiers, or Fifa…gran is brilliant at Fifa."

"Well now Marcus…it's a bit short notice for Santa but I'll see what I can do for you. You're a good lad and thank you for being honest about hitting people with snowballs"

"How do you know my name?" Marcus asked with surprise.

"Cos I'm Santa" Peggy said, puffing her chest out with pride. "I know all of you. Now I'll have a word with the elves later and see what we can do for you. Do you want a toy to take away just now?" she asked as she began rummaging in the sack beside her.

"No thanks Santa, I've got plenty of toys…give mine to a boy or girl that doesn't have as many." Marcus replied. With that he quickly hugged Santa and hopped off her lap and ran off.

"Oh, the poor wee lamb" Aggie wailed as she dabbed her eyes with a hanky.

<h1 style="text-align:center">Chapter 27</h1>

Ellie arrived at the office holding a very strong coffee. Aggie and Ann had kept her awake with their impromptu slumber party. Her only solace was that no matter how bad she felt, she was sure they were feeling worse.

"Morning everyone, happy Christmas Eve and all that. Where are we at with the case now?" She asked as she fired bacon rolls at each of them.

"Cheers Ma'am" Kent said as she tore hers open like a hungry wolf. "Sorry, I forgot to have breakfast this morning" she explained around a mouth full of bacon.

"No need to apologise Kent, I've worked with him for too long to notice" Ellie quipped as she pointed behind her to where Gavin's cheeks bulged like a hamster's as he had shoved half the roll into his mouth in one go.

"Ma'am we've confirmed that Robbie Banks was medically discharged from the Army, and he does indeed suffer from PTSD." Simpson explained, giving Kent time to chew. "He gets an army pension but it's not a lot, he is in a lot of debt and the Sheriff Officers are close to arresting his pension to pay his council tax arrears. He is in a bit of a bad financial situation."

"I see, poor lad…did security at St Enoch's find any wallets or have any reports of missing ones?" Ellie asked.

"Yes Ma'am, the cleaning staff found two empty wallets discarded near where the choir was singing, and a few other people had come forward to report theirs missing." Simpson replied.

"Well, that confirms the truth of his whereabouts I think, he's not our man." Ellie mused.

"No Ma'am…but what do we do with his theft charges?"

"I've already suggested to the fiscal that a custodial sentence would not be of benefit in this case…I'm hoping they agree and give him community service or something. I've also got Kent to have a word with a military charity that she knows, just to see if they can give him a bit of help." Ellie said as she turned to Kent who swallowed the last bit of her roll.

"Yes Ma'am, my mate says they'll be in touch with him today, just to see what he needs to keep his kids for Christmas."

"Excellent, hopefully something good can come from this." Ellie muttered. "So I think we can scratch Robbie off our list, Vikki too as she has an alibi…" Ellie said as she took their names off the board. "Where are we on Ron's life? Anything jumping out there?"

"He's squeaky-clean Ma'am." Kent responded looking at her notes. "He's never been arrested, cautioned, or even had a driving offence. He was a widower that lived a quiet life as far as I can tell. There is one thing though, he's contacted local police on numerous occasions over the last six months complaining about a stalker. I don't have the details yet though; I've requested the files, but it was that Division's Christmas night out last night so they're being a bit slow this morning." Kent explained as she rolled her eyes.

"Gav, get on to them and push, it's the only thing we have to go on just now."

Gavin picked up the phone and had a conversation that ended with "I don't care if she is being sick in the bin, one of you get those files emailed over now!" he slammed the phone down with a grin.

"With the hangover he has, that last bit will have hurt." He said evilly.

The files pinged in the joint email minutes later.

"There we go, who said that threats get you nowhere." Ellie said cheerfully as she scanned the files.

"So, the incident reports details numerous call outs as this stalker slashed Ron's tyres, cut his brakes, sent poison pen letters to the golf club making accusations about him, his cat went missing...no proof found that the person did it though...come on...tell us a name" she muttered as she scrolled through the incident reports. A name in the middle of one of the reports stopped her in her tracks.

"Bloody hell! His stalker is Sandra!"

Chapter 28

Sandra is led into the interview room; uniformed officers had been despatched to the community centre to arrest her and bring her in. She was still dressed in her elf costume and looked very calm. Ellie and Gavin sat down and started the tape.

"This interview is being conducted under caution on 24th December 2022. Present, are Detective Superintendent McVey and DI Bickerton. Sandra, can you confirm for the tape that you have been offered legal counsel and that you have refused it?"

"Yes" Sandra said in a clipped manner.

"Right, now Sandra you are aware that you have been arrested on suspicion of murder and also of attempted murder." Ellie began.

"Yes yes, your goons said all that as they manhandled me into the car. Need I remind you that I have an alibi for that speaker falling?" Sandra interrupted.

"Ah yes…you say you were caught short and had to go to the loo, yes?" Ellie asked as she looked at her notes.

"That's right, so if I didn't do one then I hardly did the other."

"Well, we don't see it that way" Ellie responded calmly.

"Especially as we have, just in the last half hour, been given the CCTV from the St Enoch's centre. Do you want to see what's on it?" Ellie asked as Sandra went a little pale.

"For the benefit of the tape we are now playing exhibit 122D, CCTV footage of the 2nd floor of the St Enoch Centre concourse." Gavin responded as he brought the footage up on the screen and played it. The footage was from the area just beside where the speaker was attached to the railings. The speaker itself was not visible. They watched as Sandra, dressed as an elf, walked quickly off to the side, and then ran back a few minutes later.

"Well, that doesn't show much, does it?" Sandra replied snidely.

"Oh, you're right, it doesn't show you actually cutting the rope. But shall I tell you what we can tell from this video? We know from the time stamp that this was exactly the time that the speaker came crashing down. We can also tell that you were the only person up there at that time as that particular bit of the concourse was closed to the public at that time. We can also tell, from plans of the shopping centre, that there are no toilets anywhere near that area, so your alibi does not hold up. Finally, Gavin will show us the enhanced image please?" Ellie asked as Gavin placed an image on screen.

"This frame has been enhanced to show what you were carrying on your way towards the speaker. Can you see what it is?" Ellie asked innocently.

Sandra looked pale and anxious but refused to answer the question.

"Shall I tell you what it looks like to us? It looks like a small knife. Incidentally we found a small knife near the place where the speaker was tampered with…someone ditched it behind a bin just beside the speaker. Forensics have matched this knife by rope particles caught in the blade as the one used to cut the speaker loose. Now shall we see if you still have the knife when you make your way back?" Ellie asked, Sandra still said nothing. Gavin played the video once more and paused it as Sandra was running back.

"We've also had this image enhanced; would you like to take a look at your hands?" Ellie asked but Sandra knew she was beat, the image showed that she had nothing in her hands.

"Why would I try to kill anyone?" Sandra blurted out desperately.

"Ah yes, I'm glad you brought that up. We've been reviewing several incident reports filed by Ron over the past six months. Complaints about a stalker making his life miserable. He named you as the stalker Sandra…I think that gives you motive, don't you?"

Sandra sat frozen, her mouth opened and closed a few times before she sighed and muttered "What's the bloody point" she then looked up at Ellie, tired and defeated. "Aye hen, he called the polis on me a few times…never could get it to stick though, I was careful you see. I um…well we were an item for a while…happiest time of my life…oh he used to take me dancing and all sorts…" Sandra said, her eyes filling with tears as she reminisced.

"But then he ended it, said I was too full on…I was furious, I just *knew* that he had found someone else. I went out of my mind, desperate to get him back…so I played a few pranks… sent letters to his golf club…threatened the woman he was dancing with at the ballroom tournament…slashed his tyres to make sure he couldn't make it to the dancing…it felt good." She admitted with a shiver of excitement. "Then I volunteered for the grotto as I knew he had signed up to play Santa…I thought if I could get to be Mrs Claus then I could spend time with him…maybe win him back…"

"But you weren't picked for Mrs Claus" Ellie surmised.

"No, Ron made sure of that! He wanted that Agnes woman instead and I had to watch as he laughed and flirted with *her* oh it made me so mad!" Sandra exclaimed.

"So, what did you do?" Ellie asked although she already knew, she could see the progression of this woman's obsession.

"I thought that if Mrs Claus had a wee accident, then she couldn't take part anymore…and I would volunteer to carry the show on…" Sandra said.

"So, you tampered with the lighting above the grotto, in the hope that when it dropped, it would land on Aggie?" Ellie said and Sandra nodded.

"For the tape can you verbalise." Gavin said to Sandra.

"Yes, I thought that would work…but I miscalculated, nearly hit Ron instead…and he was already suspicious of me." She muttered darkly.

"So, on the evening that Ron died, he stayed behind in the grotto when everyone left…was he investigating the light fixtures?" Ellie asked.

"Yes, he knows about electrics…he fitted those lights himself…when I left with Annie, I doubled back and went to the grotto to find him up a ladder examining the fittings. He saw me and accused me of tampering with it. I got so angry, didn't he see that I was trying to make things right between us?!" she shouted as she banged her fists on the table, the fire in her eyes showing the mania inside the woman. "We were arguing, he threatened to call the polis again and I lost my temper and shoved the ladder that he was still standing on. He fell...hit his head...I thought he was dead; I went to him in a panic...then he woke up and grabbed me by the throat...he was choking me...my arms flailed to find something to get him off me..." Sandra said quietly as she touched her throat.

"And you found the bell" Ellie continued.

"Yes...it was in my hand, and I hit him with it over and over until his hands dropped from my throat. I cleaned the bell with my hanky and set it down and ran out of there." She finished and looked up at them. "It was self-defence honestly."

"You may be right...but what you did to Peggy was not... that was deliberate. Why?" Ellie asked coldly.

"I was worried someone might link Ron to me, knew he had reported me to the polis before...so I had to throw you off somehow. I thought if another attempt was made on Santa's life, then the investigation would go a different way...it would give me time to think and get away. I didn't think it would hit her though" Sandra responded sulkily.

"You had no way of controlling that, you potentially could have killed three people this week! That's not self-defence Sandra, that's calculated and cold." Ellie replied. She had had enough. "Interview terminated" she muttered as she left the room without another word.

Chapter 29

It's Christmas morning in the Mitchell-McVey house and everyone is up and full of cheer. Ann was elbow deep in a turkey as Aggie read out ingredients for a new stuffing recipe to her and they each sipped some wine, neither going too mad as the hangover's were still fresh in the memory.

Kate and Ellie were enjoying a coffee and watching the two women prepare the Christmas dinner, they had offered to help but got double withering stares back, so they left the ladies to it.

"Where's Peggy?" Ellie asked, noticing the absence of the usual noisy playing with the dogs that Peggy liked to do of a morning.

"I'll show you, wait til you see" Kate said with a smirk. She led Ellie by the hand towards the living room window and pointed out to the hill in the park opposite them. It had snowed overnight again, and they watched as Peggy ran about pulling Kate's old sledge with a laughing Marcus sitting on it.

"What have I missed?" Ellie asked confused.

"All she said was that Santa had made a promise she

intended to keep" Kate said with a smile as she watched the two new pals playing in the snow.

Christmas dinner was a triumph, and everyone was full to bursting, it was now time for presents!

Aggie received a wine testing trip from Ann, perfume from Bill, CCTV doorbell from Peggy and a cashmere jumper from Kate and Ellie.

Peggy received the same wine tasting trip from Ann (Kate and Ellie warned them about their behaviour the last time!), DVDs on the cold war from Bill, and new body armour from Kate and Ellie. "It's the new model being tested on us right now…thought it might come in handy" Ellie said as Peggy looked delighted with it.

Kate got a diamond bracelet from Ellie, a walking cane that was also a sword from Peggy, the traditional selection box and jumper from Aggie, perfume from Bill and a cashmere scarf from Ann.

Bill got a case of beer from Aggie, night vision goggles from Peggy, a new tool kit from Ann "I'm hoping he will put it to good use and get my curtain pole up at last" she whispered to Kate, and a new winter coat from Ellie and Kate which he tried on and modelled around the living room.

Ann got a case of Italian wine from Aggie and Peggy, an emerald ring from Ellie and Kate and perfume from Bill.

Ellie was last and she ripped into her brightly wrapped gifts with the enthusiasm of a ten-year-old. She got a jumper similar to Kate's from Aggie, perfume from Bill, a new night stick from Peggy, a new shirt from Ann and a designer watch from Kate.

"There's one more present for you Ellie" Kate said as she

pulled an envelope from her pocket. I bought you a DNA ancestry kit...I know that you're interested in the family history...but I already sent your DNA off so that you would have the results for Christmas...and here they are." She explained as she handed the envelope over.

"Have you looked at them yet?" Ellie asked.

"Nope, I've kept them for you to open." Kate said with a smile. Ellie tore the envelope open and read the results eagerly.

"Ok says here I'm 3% neanderthal" she started as Bill sniggered.

"Probably from your side dad" she quipped. "Let's see... I'm 14% Scottish, 28% Irish, 36% French and the rest is a mixture of Danish, Swedish and Spanish..." Ellie stopped talking and went pale.

"Honey what is it? It can't be that bad to be mostly French, is it?" Kate joked as everyone chuckled.

"No...um...no there's a bit at the bottom that shows DNA links with other users of the service..."

"Ah so some 3rd cousins have come to light? Oh, or are we related to the Royals? Is King Charles your 3rd cousin twice removed?" Bill asked excitedly.

"No...it says I've got a half-brother..." Ellie said quietly.

Everyone turned to look at Bill who held his hands up in defence.

"Hey, it's got nothing to do with me! I think I'd remember if I had another sprog running about the place!"

"No, it says on maternal side..." Kate said as she read the details over Ellie's shoulder. Ellie was stunned.

"You ok sweetie?" she whispered.

"Yeah…yeah, I am…but it looks like I've got another investigation on my hands, doesn't it?" she whispered with a smile.

Epilogue

Sandra was sentenced to life for murder and for attempted murder. Her defence of not guilty by virtue of insanity was instantly dismissed as the prosecution were able to prove premeditation with the attempted murders or both Aggie and Peggy. Sandra is currently serving her sentence at HMP Cornton Vale.

Robbie Banks pled guilty to theft and was issued a community service order. He has been working with the Veterans charity to get his life back on track, he was able to see his children on Christmas day.

Peggy and Marcus became firm friends and would play video games and hide and seek whenever Peggy was free. Marcus' parents welcomed a baby girl in the summer and Peggy took a step back for Marcus to enjoy playing with his sister. Kate still catches her watching them play with a sad smile.

The charity choir raised enough money to fund a toy bank, a food bank, and a warm bank over the winter months ensuring families who needed it had somewhere to go.

Ellie spends the time between Christmas and New Year searching for details of her brother. His birth name is Ryan, but he changed it by Deed Poll to Ozzy in 2002. He was born and raised in Northern Ireland but never stayed at one address for long. The only link she has is from the DNA ancestry site, it sites his location as a camp site on the Antrim Coast. The family agree to travel over with her to help find him.

Merry Christmas Everyone

About The Author

J.a. Rainbow

J.A. Rainbow is an author based in Glasgow. She lives there with her wife and two dogs. She has always enjoyed mystery novels, especially ones that mix light-hearted humour along with drama. Although not a native Glaswegian, she is proud to live in the city and to show it off whenever she can.